BATTLE TO THE END OF DAYS

A LEGENDS OF ZYANTHIA NOVELLA

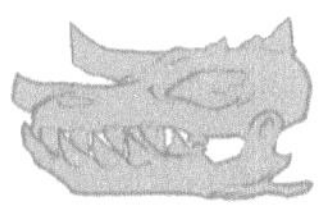

CHANTELLE GRIFFIN

Published by Chantelle Griffin in 2019

Interior layout by Chantelle Griffin
www.chantellegriffin.com

Cover artwork by Matthew K. Hoddy
www.spacepyrates.com

Catalogue-in-Publication details available
from the National Library of Australia

paperback ISBN: 978-0-6487305-3-8

Also available in hardback
ISBN: 978-0-6487305-2-1

For my sister

For all that has been before, for all the pain and sorrow, may you rise above them all. For the path less travelled brings hardship, adventure and triumph.

THE ZYANTHIAN REGION, TORDOREN

CHAPTER ONE

Siege at Odana Temple

A shattering of glass faded as the thunderous roar erupted. The blast of sorcery carved its way into Odana Temple. The shield shook down to the foundations of the building, but it held. A swarm of dragons flooded the sky, the largest Zeralden had ever seen take flight. They were headed for one place, Odana Temple. The sorcerer Keep had held against the mighty forces of the Dreshans. They took all but a few small pockets of Zyanthia. She stood in one of the last remnants, hidden away. The air ignited with the flames of dragon fire. The blaze crossed the distance between them and the temple. She wanted to move yet she stood frozen as the Dreshan Army moved in.

'Take the girl,' Arkimous shouted.

The Dreshan's stormed into the grounds of the sorcerers' Keep.

'Where? They will find her,' Senora called.

An array of smaller blasts pelted down along the side of the building. 'Anywhere but here,' Arkimous yelled above the storm of sorcery. 'I will hold the Keep.'

'Are you sure?' Senora hesitated.

'I will stay with the Keep,' he said.

Arkimous, the Otturin sorcerer and Guardian of Odana stood in a moment of calm. As the Shalough sorceress, Senora, held Zeralden's hand.

'Take the girl to the Vandragamond, they are our last chance,' Arkimous spoke.

Senora did not speak. 'Goodbye Zeralden,' Arkimous said his last words.

Then he dived into the gaping hole that led down to the central core that was Odana. The Keep rumbled and Zeralden tried to scream, but no sound came out. She peered out the window. The Dreshan Army fought against the shields protecting the Keep. Senora ran and she followed as her heart pounded. A blast echoed through the corridor up ahead. The explosion erupted into the sky and rocked the building. She lost her balance and slammed into the floor. 'Hurry,' Senora shouted.

The Dreshans were making their way across the grounds. The defences went down and she cried, 'What about Arkimous?'

'He's gone, if we stay we will share his fate,' Senora urged her onward.

The group of Otturin sorcerers along the ridge held the Keep as the walls fell around them. They ran and she struggled to keep up. Then the rumble began. Zeralden could feel it gathering speed in her mind and she wondered if it was real. 'Wait,' she called to Senora, but the Shalough sorceress would not listen. 'We have to stay.'

They stood out in the open as the dark night set in broken by the sparks of sorcery blasting at the Keep. Senora stood over her, 'You will come with us.'

A group of Shalough sorcerers appeared from hiding. They ushered her further away from the safety of Odana. The tremble that she had felt in her mind grew and the ground shook. 'We have to go now.' Senora took her to the five dragons lying in wait and placed her on the closest one. The dragon lifted into the sky. Zeralden peered back and as she did a massive beam of stallic energy shot up. It rose straight from the central core lighting up the night sky. Then the blast hit with an impenetrable wave. It hit like no other catching the dragon off-guard. It let out a cry and a blast of sorcery caught it in the sky. The dragon plummeted down and Senora screamed. It was the last sound she made.

Zeralden ran over the edge of the ravine, she tried to stop but the momentum carried her on. She panicked and turned trying to cling onto the rock. She slipped rolling down the steep surface before thudding into something hard. Voices shouted in the distance as she clung on to the living rock and cried. She wanted to say goodbye to Arkimous. The sorcerer who had given his life to protect the Keep, but there was nothing she could say. The blasts continued overhead and she stayed hidden. Then the thunderous roar of sorcery swept overhead. She could hear the Shalough scream as the Dreshan's took them down.

The cries from the dragons were worse. The sound screamed through her bones and she flinched. Then the living rock skittered down into the bottom of the ravine. She clung on with the fear of being found. The triden, a giant dark brown crab, took Zeralden back to its home. The bottom of the ravine came to life in a catacomb of caves. The triden whisked through a cave with no hint of stopping. The ceiling glowed and she clung on. The crab-like creature climbed upward along the opposite side. Then it tilted its shell at a steep angle while she slid off. Then it disappeared into the darkness.

The safety of Odana Temple was gone. Zeralden, the Angeon, was alone in the cold night air for the first time in her life.

CHAPTER TWO

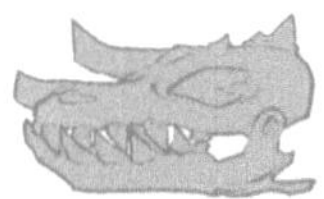

The blaze of battle

A thin layer of frost smothered the ground, as she trudged along the muddy path. The half-moon shone through the dark woods and the leaves rustled. She glanced around as the shadows moved. Shrieks filled the air from the distance and she dared not turn around. The thick haze from the smoke and sorcery crept into the dense forest. Zeralden quickened her pace. Dragons flew overhead circling in the sky as she ran. Shouts rang out before the blaze hit and a dragon swooped. It scorched the land and her auburn hair shone golden in the fiery light. Her eyes locked with the dragon and its jaw arched as the fireball flared toward her.

Zeralden gathered her sorcery and struck hard. She dived as the dragon fell from the sky. It pummelled into the open flames raging through the dense woods. She fell into the darkness as the shadows grew. Her hands slid across the rough earth bracing her fall. The dragon shrieked in pain, the harsh sounds echoed back into the ravine. She ran escaping the flames jumping through the woods. The wind blew her hair back as the chill numbed her face. A sharp metallic sound cut through the air and she clung to the bond-breaker. She drew it in the form of a dagger in the darkness.

The shadows became real as the army wrapped around her. They blocked her path away from the fire's edge. The flicking light fell across Jule Allavard as she stepped forward. The Dreshan's bond-breaker held in the form of a sword. No words were spoken as the group circled in. Zeralden took a step back toward the wall of flames. Her small frame shone near the blaze. A howl rang out from the wild heat, Gorran Valkear ran through the flames. The Dreshan sorcerer lunged forward and she twisted the blade to the side. The bond-breaker sliced through Gorran's armour. He felled with the blade and it lessened the blow. The harsh deep colour of blood welted to the surface from the wound.

'You will pay,' he glared at her.

Jule charged, and the Dreshan's blade swung high. Zeralden darted through a gap as the sorcerers all charged. Jule screamed as the blade dug deep into one of her own. Zeralden ran through the dark as the screams and shouting followed. Her heart thudded in her chest as the cold set in. She glanced up to see the small flakes of snow swarming down from the dark sky. The woods carried the echoes of chaos behind her, she did not have long. The misquew sprang silent from the forest. The riding cats blended in with the colour of night. She glimpsed the first rider through the trees and stopped. She could not return the way she came.

Dreshan sorcery flared swirling through the falling snow. The heat simmered as it hurtled toward her. She raised her arms and released her sorcery from within. It reverberated through the woods, pounding the ground so hard the earth flew upward. The confusion ran deep as a second wave blasted through. The trees fell in a circle around her. The blast gathered speed rumbling across the ground. Consuming the raging fire as it went. The smoky haze fled into the vacuum bringing with it the still of night. Zeralden had known she was different yet the impact from the blast was so great.

She dared not stay and ran as though the Dreshan Army still followed. All that came was a deafening silence that engulfed the woodland. She made her way up the hillside and stared back as the grey haze lost its grip to the beckoning day. The first rays of light stretched across from the direction of Odana. She glanced over the damage flowing into the deep ravine. The last of the snow fell as it glistened in the light. The steep edge gave above and the rocks tumbled beside her. She jumped with fright. The infant dragon summersaulted down landing with a flop. He sprang to his feet and gave a tiny roar.

She pretended to be scared, 'Please don't hurt me.'

He flew and jumped on her. She held him and glimpsed his grubby coat, 'You need a bath.'

The dragon made a whimper and gave her a quizzical look. She warmed some water and dunked him in. Before he had a chance to nip her she had dried him. She walked away and the dragon followed. He was almost as high as her knee covered in the soft coat and chubby body that marked his young age. 'You cannot follow,' she said but the dragon took no notice.

She took out a small sova bag. It became larger and she rummaged through finding a rucksack. She placed him in the sack and put it on. The dragon poked his head out and chattered away with a grumbling sound near her ear. She asked, 'Do you have a name?'

'I guess not,' she spoke to the dragon. 'What about Katholomu the dragon that stole the princess of Zyanthia. If you had the chance you would steal a princess,' she eyed the infant.

The dragon ducked in the sack then poked his head out and curled up to rest. 'Katholomu it is,' she said.

The narrow path glistened with the remnants of frost. The infant dragon snuggled in. He gave her courage even though he was still tiny, one day he would be strong and powerful. She made her way along the unused path. Each step felt like eternity as she waited for the Dreshan Army to show. She wished she could relax as the sun broke through the winter sky. It gave a welcome relief from harsh wind.

The bond-breaker Alamere remained hidden on her belt. The dagger made of heart stone, a brilliant deep sea green for Odana Temple. The sorcerer Keep had remained the heart of Zyanthia before the Dreshan Army descended.

She glanced around at a place that showed the signs of decay. The battlements were long gone, with the remnants hidden underneath the ground.

CHAPTER THREE

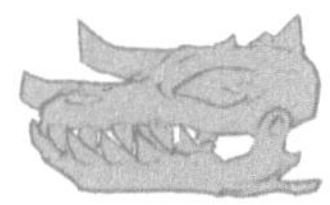

A remnant of old

The woodland opened into a small plain, as Katholomu slept. She glanced around with a sense of unease, keeping toward the edge. She trudged through the snow covering the path hidden from the direct rays of the sun. The frost covered branches swayed overhead as the wind swept through. Zcraldcn stcppcd forward and thc stonc bcncath lit up. She smiled at the sight of an old lay-line, it offered faster pace of travel. If she used it there would be a greater chance of being found. She hesitated and glanced around. Then she continued through onto the lay-line that would quicken her journey at the edge of the plain.

The faint light from the end of the lay-line beckoned up ahead. Still there was no sign of anyone. She stepped out as the dragon poked his head out of the rucksack. He jumped up kicking his legs hard against her back and she fell into the sodden earth. She cried out as a blast of sorcery pelted overhead. The heat whooshed above taking her breath away as she stumbled. Kat ran through the rocky hillside escaping her view as she fled. Dreshan soldiers followed closing the distance with a rapid pace. She turned to see Gorran's face before his sorcery ripped through the air.

Katholomu's voice carried in the void. She saw the mark of the old seal on the smooth surface and melded through the solid door. She ran into a myriad of cobwebs. Weaving their way from the ceiling and the dragon laughed. Zeralden bundled the cobwebs and threw it at the dragon. He puffed his cheeks and bellowed a tiny ball of flames. She asked, 'Where are we?'

The walls were well built and held strong. Yet they showed the damage that had gutted the old sorcerer's Keep. The corridor led to a large room hidden in the hillside.

A pebble rolled forward over the edge and hit the surface of the dark pool below. She stared down in amazement. All but the frame of the old beams remained of the once grand chamber. The murky fluid sheal flooded the void below, the potent energy sat with deathly silence. The beams were wide and she stepped out over the void as Katholomu followed. The infant dragon flew ahead landing near an open corridor. A sorcerer's voice boomed from the dark, 'Leave.'

Leathen, a pale greying sorcerer in ragged robes, stood near the small dragon. He peered out and his piercing gaze stopped at Zeralden.

The sight of the Angeon haunted him, 'Leave, there is no place for you here.'

'Wait,' she called out as she hurried along the beams. 'Who are you?'

'Did the Otturin teach you anything? Zyanthia fell. You are not welcome here,' Leathen stood his ground.

'But…' She said.

Dust shattered the silence as the seal broke from the door and Leathen shouted. He blocked the nearest exit with his sorcery, 'Leave.'

She catapulted her sorcery above the infant dragon's head. Kat screeched and ran past the sorcerer into the dark.

Shouts from the Dreshan soldiers echoed in through the chamber. Zeralden ran knocking Leathen aside. She heard his screams behind her as the soldiers blasted their way through. Then an almighty roar enveloped the passageway. Katholomu let out a high pitched shrill near an opening and she ran out into the cold air. She hurled the dragon away from the entrance. The flames hurled outward melting the snow. She clung to the dragon who wriggled out of her grasp. He gave a roar answering with a small flame near the entrance. The image of the small dragon made her smile, 'You are going to cause a lot of trouble when you grow up.'

They darted away from the old sorcerer Keep careful to stay away from the roads. The dragon's belly rumbled. She had food but the little creature would need meat. They spotted some hares in the distance and she stayed hidden while he hunted. Kat held his head high when he brought back the trophy. Zeralden made a small shield to reduce any smoke and lit a fire to cook the hare. Kat was eager to eat and watched in fascination. He let out a small whimper then puffed his cheeks. She just had time to step back as the flames roasted the hare. He scoffed down half the hare then handed the rest to her. 'No thanks,' she said.

Kat looked at her with a sideways glance then ate the rest. It did not take long for the infant dragon to become tired. She scooped him up in the rucksack and he leaned his head against her shoulder. As he slept dragon riders flew overhead. The woodland was dense and they stayed out of sight. She glanced skyward and tripped. Katholomu rolled out with a bump and told her off with a tiny roar. Zeralden rubbed the dirt off her hands. Spotting the rusty shield embedded in the mud. The ground was littered with the remains of a battle long gone.

She moved the broken shield. It revealed the skeletal forearm of a fallen warrior, and she stepped back. The infant dragon began rummaging. He flicked a gold coin into the rucksack lying on the ground, then another. She eyed Katholomu as he tugged at the remnants of a leather glove. The dragon fell backward. A small bone hurled up in the air and the jewelled ring rolled toward her. She picked it up holding it out to entice the dragon close. She held it just out of reach as she checked his markings. The pure lines of a thoroughbred marmoz confirmed her suspicions. She spoke into his ear, 'You are not supposed to collect finery for some time. Who are you little one?'

The dragon played with the ring then kicked it into

the rucksack. The shadows were growing as the sky grew dark. She needed to find shelter and picked up the rucksack with the dragon in it. A ray of small lights filtered through in the distance highlighting a small town. It would take a while to reach as she held her cloak close, wrapping it around her hands. The chill of winter settled in the air. The breeze rustled through the last of the falling leaves.

CHAPTER FOUR

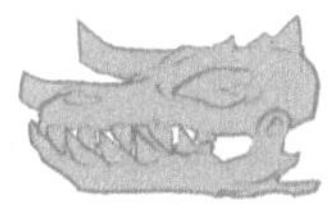

An act of mercy

She trudged through the icy wind to a tavern on the outskirts. The memory of the dragon riders clung in her mind. Voices ebbed their way through the tavern door and she hesitated. The small town of Greddin was marred by the signs of neglect. The door creaked and she wiped the grime off her boots. The mat was well worn yet the fire burned bright giving warmth to the room. The figures hunched over showing the signs of a hard life. They were unwilling to pay her attention. Zeralden could feel her skin prickle as her anxiety grew. The icy wind droned through the old wizard town rattling down the cobble street.

She reached into the rucksack careful not to reveal the dragon as she took a few coins. The snow had settled and all she could think of was a nice warm room to spend the night. The stew was hot and she made her way to an empty spot near the corner, away from the fire. Katholomu was fast asleep curled up. She patted him, and he rubbed his head against her hand. The little dragon made no sound. The wind blew hard with an icy chill as the door to the tavern opened. Two Dreshan guards made their way to the bar. As Milly and Claude the owners of the small establishment welcomed them.

Zeralden shrunk further into the corner while trying not to draw attention. The Dreshans loud voices travelled as Milly filled their mugs with ale. While they had their backs turned she scurried upstairs to her room. The window looked out over the cobble street. There was no sign of the Dreshan soldiers who followed her. Kat crawled out of the rucksack and made himself at home in front of the small hearth. The fire warmed her hands she had not slept for more than a day. She set up a tiny circular charm, the sacra seal would be enough to warn her of danger as she slept. If only she could rest as easy as the dragon did.

Her dreams were filled with flames raging across the sky. She saw Arkimous, he was trying to tell her something, but she could not hear the words. It was too late, the sacra seal woke her with a start and she knocked it on the floor. 'Hurry,' she said.

Kat shook his head, and she glared at him. She did not have time to argue as they ran into the corridor. A clambering of voices floated from the stairwell and she stopped. She turned toward a large window at the other end and leaned out. A makeshift ladder rested against the wall and she climbed down. She ran into the street as the shouts bellowed from above.

Claude appeared from around the corner, 'It's all right, follow me.'

He led her down a small alley and pointed to a path that led to a sealed entrance. Before she could ask he had vanished. She melded through the sealed door. A staircase led below the street. She hesitated then made her way along the narrow path. A small hum resonated through the wall. She passed through to the underneath of the wizard Keep. Greddin Fort hummed, yet it did not speak to her. The thick columns holding the fort above were layered with dust.

She wanted to call out, but could sense the Dreshan sorcerers above. She wandered through the underground corridors. The infant dragon followed close behind and sneezed. A voice spoke from the dark and Zeralden hid. The wizard, Frank, asked, 'What are you doing here?'

He approached Katholomu and the dragon arched his small wings in protest. Frank scooped him up as the dragon tried to fly away. Kat stared at the wizard, and Frank laughed, 'You need to be a bit older for that to work.'

He sat the infant dragon down on a soft pile of rags while he worked on the sub-station. It lay between the columns in an open space with pipes connecting through the building. The Keep looked as though it had seen better days as Frank filed back a cog. Katholomu curled up on the rags and waved his tail with delight. Frank spoke, 'So who is your friend?'

Kat's ear pricked up as he pretended not to know. 'You

were travelling with a sorceress.'

Zeralden could feel her face go red as she listened.

She stepped out of the shadows, 'How did you know?'

'All the Dreshans can talk about is a sorceress and small dragon. They say you died at the old sorcerer Keep,' he said. 'I suggest you don't stay long or the Dreshans will know.'

She asked, 'How?'

'I will tell them,' Frank answered. 'I am due to report the Dreshans in three days when my task is done. I suggest you leave before then.'

Zeralden was mortified at what she heard, yet she could not stay. She had to reach the Vandragamond. She watched the skada in silence. The spider like mechanical creatures helped to hold the tools for the wizard. Frank was at ease as the skada stayed close. She asked, 'Can I help?'

'No,' Frank spoke too loud, 'They will sense you.'

He stopped to eat a meagre lunch. She opened a small sova bag and waited for it to expand in size. She took care unwrapping a parcel and offered him some food. Frank accepted with a nod of appreciation.

He asked, 'Do you have a plan?'

She hesitated before answering, 'I am heading to the Vandragamond.'

He laughed and then stopped. 'Stay clear of the Vandragamond, they kill Dreshans and Zyanthians alike, ' he said.

She began, 'The Otturin…'

'The Otturin don't know everything,' he interrupted.

'You will have to fight them.'

She asked, 'What do you mean?'

He spoke, 'If you want the Vandragamond to listen you will have to fight. Did the Otturin tell you that? I guess not.'

Her look of bewilderment spoke for her. She did not imagine having to fight the clan that could help her.

CHAPTER FIVE

Gathering stone

Light shone in from above, it splayed across the underground room in an eerie tone. Sounds from the fort echoed down through the corridors. They filled the cavities between the columns leading down in the earth. Zeralden could sense a wizardess approaching. She scooped up Katholomu and Frank shook his head. She hoped he had made the right choice as Adia drew closer. The wizardess hesitated and spoke few words before leaving. Frank was about to settle into his work when the air whipped back along the corridor. He shouted as he knocked Zeralden out of the way. The sorcery exploded hurtling through the room at speed.

The dragon trembled behind her and stayed close. She was unprepared as she stared into the wizard's hollow eyes. Frank fell with a thud to the floor and she scrambled away. Zeralden ran amid the catacomb of columns. A blast of sorcery thundered through the air and she held the dragon tight. Katholomu glared at her, then thumped his head against hers. She let out a gasp and dropped him. Kat raised his wings and gave a roar far too load for his tiny frame. The sound echoed through the corridors. He gave her an unimpressed look as he stepped out of the way.

Zeralden was not about to be outdone by the infant dragon. She could sense the Dreshan sorcerers closing in and stared at Kat. 'This is how it's done,' she said.

The Otturin had warned her against making bond-breakers, the weapons made of heart stone. A stone formed from a combination of sorcery, the energy of the Keep and Tordoren. The crystal clear stone in the form of a sword held great power for those who knew how to use them. She held out her arms and reached out with her sorcery. The air swirled around her as the energy from the Keep rose from the ground and Tordoren. The final element called at her bidding, recognising the Angeon within. Katholomu stepped back waiting a hint of excitement flashed in his eyes.

The blades of the bond-breakers formed in her hands. They were the colour of deep blood-black for Greddin Fort. The heart stone in the blades gleamed absorbing the light from the darkness. The swords flashed as she closed in on a Dreshan sorcerer, as his body fell it turned to ash. Kat's ears pricked up and she followed his gaze. Zeralden lunged forward it was all she needed as the sorcerer fell. She transformed the blades into short daggers keeping one on her belt. She hid the other in a sova bag and ran out of the fort. She glanced back, the wizard Keep had been neglected, yet she did not want to stay. The Dreshans would know she had survived, she trembled at the thought.

Kat climbed into the rucksack as she made her way further west. Her boots kept out the icy layer covering the ground as she trudged along. The hill began to steepen as night fell she sensed a small seal nearby and followed. The wind blew against her frozen skin as the hood of her cloak blew in the dragon's face. Kat jumped down and ran toward the sealed entrance hidden in the hillside. She picked him up and they both entered. Warmth met them from inside the Keep that lay silent above it lit their way along to a small alcove.

Zeralden called out with her sorcery and the Keep answered in kind. 'Wait,' she said as Kat scurried straight into a wizardess. Elmira glanced down. 'It's been a long time since we have seen a hatchling from the Otturin,' she said.

The infant dragon scurried back. 'So much for being brave,' Zeralden remarked.

'Are you Shalough?' Elmira asked.

'Yes,' Zeralden answered.

'You are a long way from home. We cannot offer much,' Elmira said. 'If you stay too long the Dreshan's will know you are here.'

The wizard Keep was calm amidst the outside turmoil. Warm air ran up from the conduits below. It was a welcome relief from the first glimpse of winter. The Keep made no attempt to speak with her, if it did the Dreshan's would know where she was. Odana Temple had spoken to her. The absence of the Keep's company compounded her isolation. She had to find a way to the Vandragamond, yet the Dreshans had met her at every turn. She gazed down at the infant dragon who curled up in a basket on the floor. She waited for her sova bag to expand before retrieving a map. Arkimous had been a stickler for being prepared.

Zeralden hesitated as she folded out the map. The memories of her last days at Odana flooded through. 'One day you will see Zyanthia rise again,' she said to Katholomu as he slept.

The light source from the Keep shone on the map. Ollanthia home to the Tarquerin sorcerer clan was the closest. The wizard Keep Kaythar was too far way. If the Dreshans found her she would have nowhere to run. The thought made her uneasy she dimmed the light and made her way to bed.

The blanket began to slip and Kat jumped on the bed, he sniffed her face and let out a sneeze. She made a small light with her sorcery. Watching as the dragon nestled down beside her. 'You won't be able to do that when you grow up,' she said as the Kat pretended not to notice. Her mind filled with the Keep humming away in the dark. It was only just audible through the thick stone walls. The infant dragon nudged her hand and she patted him. The raging fire and cold snow filled her dreams as she tried to block them out.

The morning was filled with activity. The wizards of

the Keep worked away hidden in the hillside. She took the little dragon outside. The grounds were overgrown with the woodland showing all the signs of abandonment. Katholomu wandered out playing in the thin layer of snow. He doubled back admiring his own tiny footprints. Then wandered further out and enticed her to follow. She glanced back at the Keep. It would be wonderful to stay, yet with every moment the danger lingered. She did not want to admit it, but they would have to leave.

CHAPTER SIX

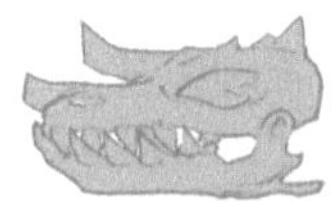

A harsh welcome

Zeralden gazed down at the paw prints from the infant dragon. She made her way along the trail through the woods. A chill swept past as the wind gathered speed and she lost sight of Katholomu. A rustle came from the undergrowth and she peered through the web of branches. A small dragon peered up, yet it was not hers. It backed away at a slow pace with a low growl. Katholomu shrieked behind her and ran as the flames flared into the sky. Shouts rang out through the woods and she ran after the infant dragon. The roar came through the sky as the dragon riders followed.

She ducked down into an alcove marking the beginning of a small cave. The infant dragon stayed close by her side. She held out the sacra seal near the entrance. It created a barrier concealing them from the outside. The seal of sorcery allowed them to see out and it would be difficult to detect. It was a small comfort as the dragon peered out, not making a sound. Kat's wings flared at the sight of the adult dragons flying overhead. 'Not today,' she whispered, 'When you are older you can fight.'

The dragon gave her a mournful look in an attempt to contain his eagerness.

They were far enough away from the wizard Keep, yet still some distance from Ollanthia. It was going to be a long day as she settled in. If she could not leave then she would rest. Katholomu watched on as the sky grew dim. The infant did not falter as he glared outward. His eyes kept searching the distance even as he curled his tail around to rest. Darkness called with the icy wind. Zeralden stepped out as all trace of the dragons and their riders had gone. She picked up the infant dragon in the rucksack. He let out a small protest before accepting. Allowing his head to poke out he brushed his head against her ear.

A low rumble came from the rocky hill and a misquew emerged from its den. The riding cat blended into the night, only its eyes shone bright. It sneezed and the warm air filtered through the cold breeze. She held out her hand and beckoned the misquew to come closer. The creature did so permitting her to ride. It clung to the rocky hillside away from the dense woodland. It gave her time to search the darkness. The only movement came from the chill that wrapped its way around the icy ground. The rocky hill turned into a field of snow covering the grass beneath. It marked the edge of the woodland. They were close to

Ollanthia, yet there was still some way to go.

She slid down from the misquew, taking out a piece of dried meat for the creature to eat. Katholomu protested and she broke off a piece. The infant dragon grasped it before swallowing it whole. The hour was late as she peered through the dark, to see a thin trail of smoke rising from a cluster of weathered, wooden buildings. They were still far from the grounds of Ollanthia, yet the early night had served her well. Katholomu followed her through the still night air. The chill of winter crept along her fingers. She gave a hesitant knock and no one answered.

The door swung ajar and she peered through the cottage calling out. The sweet smell of food wafted from the kitchen and the infant dragon ran toward it. A scream filled the void then all went silent. She entered the room to find a grey-haired woman with a large frying pan. The pan was held between her and the dragon. 'It's okay,' Zeralden said.

'I know who you are,' the old wicca woman glared. 'Keep that creature out of my kitchen.'

Zeralden picked up Kat, 'I was wondering...'

'You can stay in the barn and leave in the morning. We don't want anything to do with your kind,' the old woman spoke.

A tall scrawny lad showed her to the barn where a fire kept the animals warm. She thanked him and made herself a bed near the hearth. The infant dragon gave her a mournful look and his tummy rumbled. 'Don't be greedy,' she said as she patted him. He gazed at her warm blankets and curled up in them. The wind picked up hurling itself against the barn. She was relieved to be near the warmth of the fire as she laid down to rest. The embers lowered and the dragon wriggled free, he nudged a thin log on the fire and blew. The flame whirred from his mouth and she jumped as it startled her.

She picked him up and gazed into his eyes, 'You are not supposed to breath fire.'

Katholomu stuck out his tongue in a defiant protest.

As they lay in the blanket the infant dragon coughed and she stared at him. 'Don't set the bed on fire,' she said.

The last thing she needed was an infant dragon that could breathe fire. Yet she did not have the heart to leave him. She gazed at his small face snuggled beside her. They were both far from home.

The morning light broke too soon and she remembered the old woman's words. She tucked the bedding away into a sova bag and shrank it down so it would fit in her pocket. The last of the fire's warmth filled the barn as she reached for the door. A fresh layer of snow had covered the ground below. Kat sat snug in her rucksack as she closed the door behind them. The barn had offered a welcome sleep and she gazed to the great hill on the horizon. There lay the sorcerer Keep Ollanthia. It was the home to the Tarquerin the smallest sorcerer clan to grace Zyanthia.

She trudged through the shallow snow and hoped that no more would fall to block their path. The early morning wind howled. As though taunting her as she crossed the open fields. The rocky path lay along the edge of the hills.

The snow only just touched it leaving a trail of fine rock to follow. The Tarquerin were the closest to the Otturin who lived along the Menna Range. Not all the Otturin had made it to the safety of Odana Temple. For its many barriers the stories had filtered through. Leaving her to wonder what would be left of Ollanthia.

CHAPTER SEVEN

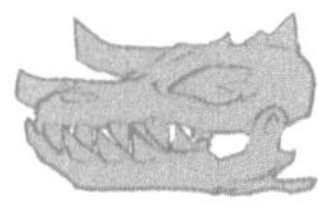

A burden from the past

The grounds of the Keep wrapped around the low-lying hill. Inviting Zeralden with a calm response as the wind dissipated. A barren patch marked the edge of an end node, the outer rim of the Keep. The sorcerer's stone shone with a tarnished surface. Small grooves ran around in a faint pattern. The infant dragon bounded onto the grassy edge and ran along the stone. Katholomu screeched and flew to the edge. She placed her hand to the stone, yet she sensed nothing. Kat gazed at her with wide eyes. 'I believe you,' she said to sooth the dragon.

She made her way across the courtyard as the sun shone warming up the chill of winter. The Keep hummed away with steady rhythm, she sensed it rather than heard it. The sound was too faint, hidden far beneath the ground. The sun's ray belied the chill carried in the air as she kept her hands covered. The fallen snow filled the edge around the sorcerer Keep yet the path was clear. She strode past the columns guarding the entrance to the courtyard. The sound of her footsteps echoed in the silence yet no one greeted them. She glanced around at the worn stone marking a once grand entrance. Katholomu followed curling his tail around as he lay in the warmth of the sun.

She entered the foyer towering above in the darkness. Before the lights trickled on providing an ambient glow. Heddwyn glided from the shadows the old Tarquerin sorcerer had a hollow face. The white wisps of hair escaped from around his high collar. He took the image of the sorceress in his stride. He welcomed her with a greeting that channelled his voice through the empty foyer. He paid little attention to Katholomu. The infant dragon wandered ahead through the wide empty corridors. Zeralden followed in Heddwyn's lead as the Keep remained silent. A weathered edge hung over the pearl walls showing the age of the building.

Kat sneezed sending a cloud of dust into their path. She managed to avoid stepping into the infant dragon as he darted behind her. Heddwyn showed her to a spacious room with a balcony overlooking the falling hillside. She let in the cold chill to glimpse the path she had taken. Yet as she peered in the distance she could not find a trace. She glanced back to see Katholomu curled up asleep on the bed. The dragon was so small and she almost forgot he was real as he stayed so still. The balcony offered a view back to the sorcerer Keep. She caught sight of a figure through a window then it vanished.

The small sova begs in her pocket held all her possessions. She expanded one next to the infant dragon. He lifted his head with interest before settling down. Zeralden held the bond-breaker in her hand. She hesitated then returned it to her belt. Its twin stayed in the bag and she reached in. 'Here,' she said to Kat, 'keep it safe.'

He reached out and to her amazement tucked it underneath him.

There was little more she could do as she consulted the map. It would be a difficult journey north-west to Kaythar the wizard Keep.

She would have to gather her strength and rest. 'I wish I could sleep as much as you,' she patted Kat who twitched his ear in recognition.

Shadows peered across the room as the sky grew dark and she let the infant dragon be. A faint smell wafted up from the kitchen. To her surprise the great hall was well lit with a small gathering. The empty space made the hall appear larger than it was. Heddwyn offered her a chair and she accepted. They gazed upon a vast view of the valley, that gave an eerie silence and let the darkness fill the void.

It was not the Ollanthia she had heard of from Arkimous. The Otturin had been a young man when the Dreshans invaded. His tales had been full of life and a vibrancy that did not exist in the world outside Odana Temple. An awkward silence hung over the table and she felt the sorcerers watch as she ate. Heddwyn invited her on a tour of the Keep and she accepted. It was a welcome relief as she left the great hall behind. The empty rooms and layers of dust gave the building a sense of abandonment.

Warm air swept up from the Keep below. It protected them from the winter chill emanating from the windows. Heddwyn showed her around the Keep. To her relief there were still areas that were well looked after amidst so much gloom. She tried not to show her surprise at the contrast as he kept moving. Perhaps another time she would say something. The Tarquerin were but a memory of what they once were. She glanced around the vast vacant rooms. The stark contrast hit home with a sadness she did not expect.

The chamber was almost empty. It had been rumoured to have the greatest treasures of the sorcerer clans. Zeralden gazed upon the flawed Orb. The breaks shone with a feathered spray of light. It almost reached the centre, marking the Orb close to its end. The hilt of a bond-breaker lay at the centre of the room. It made the most prominent piece in the collection. She appreciated the perseverance of the Tarquerin yet the reality still shocked her. Heddwyn had taken care to avoid the paths that led to the levels below and she did not ask. If she made a connection with the Ollanthia the Dreshans could find her. It was a risk she was willing to avoid.

Zeralden made her way to her room. The small lights from the Keep glowed along the corridor guiding her way. The room was warm and she peered around searching for Kat yet there was no sign of him. She called in a soft voice hoping for reply, yet still she heard nothing. She sat on the bed resting her weight on her hands. Her fingers caught on a rip in the fabric. She stood to find the marks left by the infant dragon hidden in the folds of the cover. Katholomu was gone.

CHAPTER EIGHT

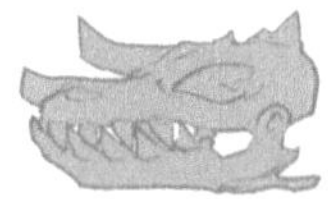

Fall of the illusion

Panic caught in her throat as she held back a scream. Zeralden hurled back the covers. There was no sign of the bond-breaker or the infant dragon. She became frantic heading toward the door, the building lay silent as she searched. There was no sign of Heddwyn or the dragon. Each corridor led to nothing, she thudded her hands against the wall in frustration. She had to find the Katholomu and the bond-breaker yet the Keep remained silent. She could not communicate with the Keep. If she did, then she could count down the time before the Dreshans arrived. It was not a choice she wanted to make.

She reached her senses out. Her sorcery wove through the empty spaces calling out in her mind. The power of the Angeon grew within her. She had spent her life training for the day she would have to choose the path she would walk. The Otturin had been adamant that until that day she would not be strong enough to fight. Yet she was no longer in the safety of Odana Temple. Her sorcery sensed a faint signal sealed deep beneath. She caught an image of the infant dragon calling out and hand holding a blade. The image was enough as she opened her eyes.

Zeralden gazed at the sealed doors. They led down below the habitable area of the Keep. She placed her hands on the cold solid door, it stood her height again as she peered up at the seal. The small glow came to life spreading out in a web over the door. 'Do not break a sealed door unless you are prepared for what lay before,' she said.

She repeated the words in her mind and held out her hands, 'Rise.' The door shook, and she shouted, 'Rise.'

The seal began to part and she shouted the word again as it fell. A gust of wind blew the doors out. As the pressure dissipated she shielded herself with her sorcery. It created an aura that faded as the room fell silent.

She held the dark blade of the bond-breaker at an angle. Ollanthia Keep remained silent as it watched her. She could sense it stir below in the imbenik chambers. Its thoughts escaped fleeting past, the images branched out brushing through her mind. It was not what she had wanted to see. She glimpsed the infant dragon again and ran. The image faded as shouting crept along the corridor and she wondered if she was too late. The thought drained the colour from her face as she ran. A tiny high-pitched squeal rang out from Katholomu.

The chamber appeared empty except for the infant

dragon backing up against the altar. Zeralden entered, she was knocked into the air and held onto the blade with a tight grip. The force tried to rip it from her grasp, yet she held it as her fingers turned white. A trail of sorcery streamed around her lifting her from the ground. It faded into a void of nothing. The void left an image in the periphery of her vision. She grappled trying to concentrate yet the void remained empty. Her fingers were losing their grip as the whirlwind pulled her in. She was blind in the world without dreams, yet she lashed out with the bond-breaker.

It slashed across the real world and the other. The blade wept as blood soaked the edge, and she hit the floor. She gazed up and saw the outlines of the sorcerers out of phase with the real world. They were hidden between time and space, in a world without dreams. Her bond-breaker shone a deep dark red and the other blade shone in response to her call. Idris held the blade in an arc, close to her side as she rushed in. The two worlds met as the blades linked through the air. The bond-breaker broke free from the Tarquerin sorceress. Idris screamed across the void and the blade hurled into the altar with a thud.

It hit the stone above the infant dragon's head and Kat growled. He bit the hilt and a small flame beamed down igniting the blade. It reached the altar and flared to life. The energy criss-crossed a web of brilliant light that flickered up the walls. The void collapsed as the two worlds collided in the chamber. Ollanthia stirred from the deep as the building rumbled. The Tarquerin sorcerers stepped away as the Keep sprang to life. Zeralden gripped the blade and pulled it free of the altar. The web of light spread down toward the floor and the Tarquerin ran. Katholomu let out a low growl. She could sense Ollanthia from the deep as the energy rose beneath them.

The pace quickened and she placed the bond-breakers away in dagger form. She ran and Kat followed. She could sense the Tarquerin heading toward higher ground. She ran toward the open courtyard. Her ears thudded with the sensation from the Keep. The stallic energy rose up from the central core. She could see the courtyard and made it to the foyer. Heddwyn stood in her way. Kat ran into her as she came to a stop, the Tarquerin sorcerer raised his arms and she flinched. The blast of sorcery was too close and she only just had enough time to block. Heat emitted from the collision just beyond her.

She winced and the infant dragon spread his wings. Katholomu steadied his weight and hurled through the barrier of competing sorcery. He attacked and Heddwyn slammed Kat to the ground. The infant dragon slid along the hard surface. Zeralden strengthened her blow sending the barrier toward Heddwyn, it was too slow. He attacked again. She held the barrier in place as the stallic energy came closer to the surface. As Heddwyn moved again she slid the barrier sideways on its edge. The force struck behind her, she picked up Katholomu and ran for the door. Heddwyn shouted behind her as she gripped the infant dragon tight. Kat's head bobbed and he let out a little squeak.

It was only warning she had. The stallic energy flooded

to the surface and she held the dragon high. The energy came to the surface in waves pulsing up along the outer walls of the building. If the Dreshans did not know she was here they would now. The stallic energy lit the night sky. It pummelled upward in a single spire reaching to the stars above. The infant dragon squirmed free and sat on her head. His tail curled around tickling her neck. He let out a loud squawk. 'Yes, you did that. Next time warn me,' she said.

He leaned over and gave her an upside down quizzical glance. She touched his nose, 'Yes, you.'

CHAPTER NINE

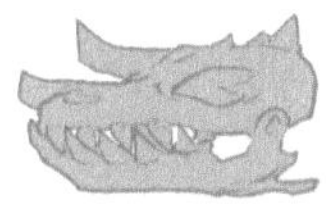

To chance or dare

Zeralden took shelter in a small cave the last remnant of a former Keep. The sacra seal kept, offered a level a safety she was willing to trust as exhaustion set in. Kat inspected the blanket before curling up beside her. The infant dragon had the warmth of a tiny furnace wrapped in a thick layer of toughened skin. He rubbed his head against her arm. The day was beautiful and calm, but if she did not rest sleep would catch her. She woke to the howl of the wind. Calling along the hillside as it rushed through the rocky terrain. A shadow hungover her, and she glanced up. Strachan held out his hand with a slither of apple. The infant dragon ate the small offering.

The Dreshan sorcerer was not much older than she. Zeralden stood up, 'How did get in?'

He glanced over to the sacra seal, 'I wasn't looking

for you.'

He stroked the infant dragon and Katholomu purred. She could sense sorcerers approaching from the tunnels. She gazed at the entrance to the cave with the open sky. 'I wouldn't go that way,' Strachan said.

She glared at the Dreshan sorcerer, his calm composure irritated her. Voices trailed toward them from the tunnels.

She raised her sorcery from within and he laughed blocking her attempt. Strachan continued to play with the infant dragon. Kat appeared completely oblivious lapping up the attention. Zeralden stepped toward him, 'I wouldn't do that if I were you.'

The sounds drew close through the tunnels there was no time to waste. The energy of the Angeon rose calling from beneath the surface. A momentary glance of fear was the last expression on Strachan's face. The energy catapulted through the air whipping down the tunnels. He flew across the cave with the impact and she picked up the infant dragon. Katholomu purred louder near her side.

She ran toward the entrance of the cave and faltered. The hillside swarmed Dreshan soldiers caught off guard by the blast. The debris showered them as the air settled and she ran along the hillside. Kat called out in a short shrill pitch as he lifted his head to the sky. She glanced up as the giant dragon swooped. He skidded through the dirt and the infant dragon squirmed free. Kat jumped onto the adult dragon. She clambered on as the first blast sparked toward them in a fiery arc. Her sorcery shielded them and the dragon took off with a jolt through the icy wind. She clung onto the dragon's main near his shoulders. His rough skin showed the faint remnant of scaring down his limbs.

Night fell with the shadows creeping in. It was then that the glints among the open sky gave away the dragon riders in the distance. Zeralden's heart beat in her stomach, 'We have to land.'

The great beast swerved and she lost sight of the dragon riders. He came down to fast and sprang up with a jolt. She lost her grip and tumbled into the snow. The dragon wedged himself into the ground. His head appeared above and he stared at her. She ran across and slid down his side.

The dragon crawled deep in the ground. Marking the entrance to his home then curled up to sleep. One eye opened as the dragon gazed at her and he spoke, 'Angeon.'

'Yes,' she answered. 'Who are you?'

'Hemreck,' the dragon spoke and closed his eye.

Kat ran near her legs and gazed up he ran down the tunnel and stopped waiting for her. A hollow drone emanated from below. Her senses picked up the stallic energy creeping up walls. 'Katholomu,' she shouted and the infant dragon backed away.

She ran toward him and he reached out as she lifted him in the air, 'Stay with Hemreck.'

He gave her a quizzical look and the energy crackled below. Kat's ears twitched at the disturbance. He ran toward the old dragon whose snoring rumbled down the tunnel. Kat stopped at the entrance and waited. She made her way the tunnel, the grey stone walls unravelled. The noise filled her ears, a low tumultuous circling motion from deep beneath. She peered down into the depths where the staircase led down. Sparks crept from below with startling speed, almost silent except for the low rumble.

Zeralden made her way toward the edge of the gaping pit. It was the closest she had been to the central core. The inner working of Odana Temple had been off limits. She found herself caught between fear and amazement. Curiosity kept her close to the edge and she peered over. A surge of the stallic energy thrashed to the surface in a spray of light, and she fell. Her hands waved in the air catching nothing. She sank as the stallic energy whirled around. It pulled her down into toward the central core. The outer shell wore the signs of a shattering long before. Sorcerer's stone corroded around the creases allowing the stallic energy to flow.

Panic began to rise as she sensed what lay behind the fragile shell. She shouted, yet the sound was swallowed in the energy rising form the core. She closed her eyes for a brief moment floating inside the central core. The lead driven into Tordoren lay in pieces to the side of the core. All that remained was a distant memory of what had been as the stallic energy shot upward. The voice of the Keep was gone, the core destroyed. Sadness swept over her, she was inside a silent tomb. Stallic energy flowing from the open wound left behind. Zeralden gathered her strength, the Angeon rose to the surface. She took aim at the wound in the earth and willed it to heal.

The stallic energy continued its path to the surface. The last remnants of the energy swept past in a random state. She focused again, calling the Angeon from within. The sorcery of old tied her to Tordoren. A surge came surrounding her in a sphere of sorcery that lit up the empty space. Then she let go. It catapulted toward the strands of stallic energy rising from the deep. It smashed into the shell with the collision. The stallic energy wrapped around as the shell collapsed in the deep. The force struck pulling her down. She screamed into an oblivion that consumed the sound.

She thrashed against the hold taking her downward. Her arms flailed as they reached nothing. The shell compressed as it broke apart. Shards rained toward the open wound in the deep. Her hand reached out and she grabbed on. She floated just above the horizon of the void as the shell disintegrated below. Darkness set in and she relaxed on the ledge overlooking the fresh scar below. Her heart pounded in her ears and she took a deep breath as the spinning slowed. Cool air brushed against her skin as the dull rumble of the tunnels set in.

CHAPTER TEN

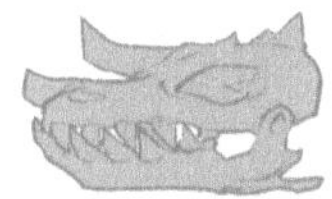

Into the heart land

Relief washed her fears away, yet still she stood staring down into the darkness. It was the first central core Zeralden had seen, the image haunted her from the depths. She made her way up the stairs and Katholomu greeted her as she picked him up. If she ventured back the Dreshans would be waiting on the surface. She pulled out a small device as the infant dragon settled in the rucksack. A small circular talik, it fit in her palm and she opened the lid. The tunnels led further west in the direction of Kaythar Keep.

Her sorcery formed a pale light, just enough to make her way in the dark. Carvings in the old sorcerer's Keep cast flittering shadows along the walls. The hollow drone from the air rushed through, crept down the tunnel. Exhaustion set in and they made a small camp hidden away. Kat arched his back surveying the place, he returned and stared into her eyes. A small sound escaped his mouth and she realised he was trying to speak. She asked, 'What are you saying little one?'

Kat raised his paw and he tried again, 'Home.'

It was tiny but audible, she patted his head, 'I guess you could say that.'

The infant dragon seemed content with her response and curled up to rest.

Zeralden woke to nothing the place was as it had been. Dark, dry, and almost void of sound. The infant dragon scurried ahead along the corridor. The vents echoed signs of life from above and she raced to catch up. The ground opened into a small cave, water dripped from the ceiling into a tiny creek. A slow trickle filtered sound through the cave as they walked on taking care not to clip. Katholomu bounded into the stream splashing water everywhere. Then he scurried over to be picked up. She used her sorcery to dry him and Kat was not impressed yet he snuggled close as they carried on.

Light beamed down through the entrance to the cave and she hesitated. They were close to the cobble road. She glanced over the rim at the village in the distance. 'Are you ready?' She asked the dragon who was fast resting the rucksack.

She pulled the heavy hood over. She stepped out into the snow that has settled around the edges. A criss-cross of tracks lay across the road and a cart passed her by, laden with goods. It travelled toward the village below. Zeralden strode onward keeping her hands covered in her coat. The infant dragon had rested low in the rucksack hidden from view as she kept to the edge of the road.

The morning call from the birds filled the sharp air and carried on the breeze. The last of the woods broke into a scattering of fields on the outskirts and she was in the open. Yet hiding had brought attention and she needed to make it to Kaythar Keep. She increased her pace toward the village. A fresh layer of snow shone over the grass that still clung on in glimpses underneath. The road was worn, but the timber and stone buildings were well kept. The houses had a fresh coat of whitewash covering the walls. A cart rolled by and she caught sight of the sorcerers walking in the distance. They were Dreshan.

Her heart beat filled her head and she only just managed to stay calm as she peered around. The village was nestled away and she could do was hope. The day was early. She kept to the shadows making her way through the village square was up ahead. The statue stood above the square. There in the depths of Zyanthia looming over her was the image she dreaded. The Dreshan Emperor set in stone. Every instinct told her to flee yet she was drawn to the centre. The shadow from spread over her from the early morning light, and she gasped. 'Beautiful isn't it,' a Dreshan sorceress spoke behind her.

'Yes,' Zeralden spoke as her thoughts raced.

She wanted to scream but she was caught between fear and awe. The place filled her with a hollowed dread. On the surface she gave a smile and the sorceress let her be. It was too close, yet she strode on toward the out-skirts. Shouting rang out as the cart pulled up near the gaol. She could sense the sorcery as the Arthrose sorcerer was beaten. The captive stared at her before she could look away. He began to shout at her. She turned her head, as her heart raced and tried to remain calm. She made it past the building and the words rang out as the captive shouted, '…Angeon.'

It was the only word that came through in the moment of silence. She pretended not to notice, and quickened her pace. A cart echoed behind her, yet there was no sign of being followed. The rucksack moved and Katholomu jumped out landing on a stand of vegetables. The board tipped and the infant dragon scampered. The vegetables crashed to the ground. Her face went pale as the store holder shouted, 'Thief!'

He spotted the infant dragon and shouted again. The Dreshan sorcerer's circled in and she glanced around as more came.

Kat ran toward her keeping his eyes locked on the group. His tail curled high and every muscle tightened. It was the only warning Zeralden had. A blast struck in an arc, it whipped through, leaving a trail of the air caught alight. She struck back and the ground shook. The arc pummelled into the buildings in a semi-circle. She swung picking up the dragon. She charged toward a weakness in the group of sorcerers. A searing pain filtered through her back as she blasted her way through. The group closed its ranks too late. The second blast hit the Dreshan sorcerers.

Zeralden paled as she heard the screams and ran. The charred rim of her cloak caught her and she stopped. Yet she did not want to look as the pain set in. The plains broke into a wood land covering the low hillside and she kept away from the path. When the cobble road was almost out of view she slowed and the infant dragon jumped down. His coat was covered in smoke, she had forgotten about him. She scooped him up and he purred rubbing his head against hers.

CHAPTER ELEVEN

An unwanted guest

A chill wind ran through the woods howling as the sun swept down upon a winter's day. Zeralden leaned back on the snow and concentrated on healing her wound. The infant dragon took the opportunity to curl up on her stomach and rest. She wanted to move him but it would break her concentration. Kat declined to notice the discomfort he caused. The early wind settled yet she could not stay. She changed her cloak putting the old one into the sova bag. It shrank into a tiny pouch and she hid it away. Kat ran through the soft snow eager to move on, she could not blame him. She rubbed her arms and held the hood close so she could glance around.

An eerie glow filtered through the fog wafting amid the trees. A bird screeched out from above. The leaves held on in a final scattering through the woods. She stayed clear of any trail following the infant dragon's lead. The sun rose marking the middle of the day and she peered around, 'Where are we?'

Katholomu glanced back, Zeralden had covered their tracks. She was starting to wonder if that had been a mistake. She removed the small circular device and opened the case. The talik showed a faint signal. 'This way,' she spoke.

The woods became dense spreading shadows along the ground. Kat remained close as the branches rustled. A movement caught her eye and the fog thickened as it gathered around the edges. Kat's ear pricked up. A faint sound carried on the wind louder than the swaying branches. She took a step back and Tavion covered her eyes, 'Don't look.'

She exclaimed, 'What?'

The ground fell away beneath them and she heard Kat screech.

Darkness set in and the Arroada sorcerer, Tavion, stood back. She peered up at the solid earth that trapped them beneath the surface. Muffled sounds pierced through the tiny holes leading down. It became louder and the distant rumbling of sorcery filtered into the void. 'You made a powerful enemy,' he whispered.

She went pale. 'Not me,' he said.

They listened as the sounds from above grew closer, they were right above. Then she heard Jule shouting over the noise. The Dreshan sorceress was so close, Zeralden froze to the spot.

Tavion waited as the sounds echoed in the shadows. She noticed the scars running along his shoulder and their eyes locked. He reached out his hand and she followed. The tunnels were rough and sturdy, their small lights guided the way. An array of tunnels led into a larger space that greeted them. She glanced above to the largest sacra seal she had seen. It loomed overhead embedded in the ceiling. She stepped on the floor underneath and it gave a small glow. She gazed down to see the second sacra seal a mirror image of the one above. They were perfectly aligned.

If it were not for the seals the place would appear ordinary. The plain tunnels carved into the ground wound around. She took care on the rough steps and peered up at the elegant columns on the great hall. She glanced back and the rough narrow stairs were still there. Tavion smiled at her astonishment. The great hall hidden well below bustled with life. She watched the Arroada in amazement. The place was in complete contrast to the world above. She spoke her thoughts aloud, 'Is this real?'

'Yes,' Tavion spoke before helping himself to a drink and a warm bread roll.

She asked, 'Where do you get food?'

'We have friends,' Tavion said. 'Not everyone likes the Dreshans.'

Zeralden frowned at the short response. She knew what happened to people who defied the Dreshan Occupation. The smell of warm bread appealed and she sat down on the bench. The infant dragon ran out from underneath her coat. He perched himself near the fire. He fluffed his mane and gave a soft purr. Tavion patted his back and Kat lost his balance. He bound over the sorcerer for comfort.

Tavion asked 'What did you do to get the attention of the Dreshan's?'

She gazed down at the infant dragon that held out his paw to the Arroada sorcerer. 'I left Odana Temple,' she explained.

He sprayed his drink over the infant dragon, and Kat ran toward the hearth. Tavion laughed at the sight then calmed his thoughts, 'You did what?'

She could feel her face grow hot, 'I left Odana Temple.'

'Forgive him for not recognising the Angeon,' Aretta spoke.

The Arroada sorceress had a thin streak of grey hair. Tavion became quiet. 'You are far from home,' Aretta continued.

'I am heading to the Vandragamond,' Zeralden responded.

'You won't find anything there, they let Zyanthia fall,' Aretta said. 'Our own kin left us, and everyone to rot.'

'The Otturin…' She spoke.

'Do not know much about the Vandragamond, yet sell them dragons,' Aretta said.

She interrupted while gazing at the tiny sleeping dragon. Aretta asked, 'Have you passed the final test?'

'I don't know what you mean,' she responded.

Aretta burst out laughing, 'You would know if you had.'

Zeralden remained calm on the outside, yet the

tension showed. Katholomu kept her company as the Arroada proceeded to talk into the night. The Otturin had always made it clear that she was the Angeon. She was caught between wanting to ask Aretta and remain silent. Tavion rounded the corner and faced her down the corridor, 'There you are.'

'Yes,' she responded with exasperation.

He leaned up against the wall looking rather pleased. 'Don't let the Dreshans get you before the final test.'

She glared at him in annoyance. Tavion laughed then let out a cough, 'Sleep well Angeon.'

She gave him a stern look, 'Thank you.'

The response was short. She entered the small room shutting the door behind her. A small glow emanated from along the edge of floor, yet there were no obvious signs of a Keep. Scratching began at the door she had forgotten the infant dragon. Kat put his paw in as she opened it, then flew past toppling onto the bed and curled up into a neat ball.

CHAPTER TWELVE

Redemption

Darkness filled the void as she called out but there was silence. Katholomu's muscles were tense and the absence of the Arroada kept her on edge. She knocked again yet there was no reply. The corridor stretched far into the Keep. She sensed an Arroada approaching from a distance. Bardrick, a gruff man with a build to match ran toward her, 'Zeralden.'

A low rumble roared between them and the ground shook with the impact. The earth ruptured and she ran. Blasts echoed from above. The heat from the sorcery seared through the dust filled air.

Kat darted ahead and she followed, another blast shattered through, knocking her down. Her hands hit the hard ground, taking her fall. Her lungs hurt. A blazing flash of light sparked whirling along the corridor and she turned. A gaping hole opened to the sky. She headed toward the opening. To the sight of the Arroada as the Dreshans swarmed around in an arc. The army massed from two sides condensing in mid-stream. Then the screams reached her. 'Tordoren forgive me,' she spoke, and stepped out.

Zeralden opened her arms wide and the ground thudded with a deafening wave. It moved at an unstoppable pace. The Dreshans faltered in its wake and the Arroada took ground standing strong. She stepped forward in full view of the Dreshan Army and began to chant. 'Fall to the Prophet, fall the Angeon; fall to Tordoren,' she said. She raised her hands and shouted, 'Fall.'

The wind ceased and a creak began. Then another from the deep and the ground opened to form a crevasse. It fractured in front of the Dreshans and spread in both directions.

The army attacked. The crevasse consumed the sorcery in the void before it had a chance to reach her. Bardrick stood in the front line as the Dreshans dispersed unwilling to let go of the day. He held out his hand to stop her as she approached. He waited as the snow fell hiding the damage, then turned toward the exposed tunnels. 'If you chase them we will not have any peace,' he said.

She stopped, 'They know you are here?'

'Yes,' Bardrick answered. 'It's an unspoken truce, until someone breaks it.'

She asked, 'Did I cause this?'

He laughed, 'It was overdue.'

She nodded and watched. The Arroada mended the walls allowing the earth to thicken in place. It appeared the same as before yet the crevasse still marked the ground. It resembled a scar in the landscape marking the lower edge of the hillside. Katholomu entangled himself around her feet and almost tripped her up. The infant dragon purred to see her and she picked him up. Shouting erupted from below and she made her way down the narrow staircase.

The glow highlighted the steps. She ran her fingers against the rough surface of the wall. Zeralden squinted in the light, the large room was well lit and it took her by surprise. Signs of the Keep marked the columns of the great hall as she glanced up in awe. Then the shouting broke through her distraction. Bardrick hit Aretta before she could reach them. 'What are you doing?' Zeralden demanded as she glared at Bardrick.

'It is not your concern,' he responded in a firm tone.

'You cannot do that,' she blocked his path.

'Aretta nearly cost you your life,' Bardrick said.

'I can look after myself,' she replied.

His expression changed. 'We have survived here for more than a decade without the Angeon. We will be here after you are gone,' he said.

Zeralden went pale, 'I will free Zyanthia.'

'You have to make it to the Vandragamond first,' he said and left.

She did not know whether to be angry with him or not. Tavion interrupted and led her away before she could decide. She asked, 'What did Aretta do?'

He hesitated and whispered, 'She let the Dreshans know you are here.'

'But…' She spoke and Tavion interrupted.

'She was scared, we all are,' he said.

It was not the answer she wanted to hear as she watched Tavion leave. A few glances headed her way. The Arroada set out reinforcing their fragile stronghold.

The tunnels that led further down were a short distance away. She ventured down. Still there was hardly any sign of the Keep as she reached out, yet she was convinced it was there. The outer rim shimmered as she had watched the Dreshans leave. She wondered if they would return. Kat followed bounding down the stairs as he went. She stopped and he bowled into her with a squawk of delight. The thin glow of light radiated upward lining the walls. She leaned against the side of the corridor it was warm to the touch.

She went down further stepping into a barren foyer void of life. The warmth emanating from the floor made her stop. Beneath her feet a large sacra seal wound its way in a circular disc covering the foyer. The Keep sensed her movement and called from below. Only this time the voice was strong. It filled her mind and she gripped her ears, yet it did nothing to block the sound. The Keep called again with a warning. That filled her heart with dread and colour washed from her face. Run and hide little Angeon the Dreshans are coming. The words filtered into her mind.

She ran as the Keep laughed in torment, sensing her plight. She ran so hard she knocked Tavion against the wall. 'Hey,' he exclaimed.

'They're coming,' she repeated. 'They're coming, I have to leave.'

Tavion asked, 'What are you talking about?'

'The Keep said the Dreshans are coming, I have to leave,' she explained.

Tavion went silent before responding. 'The Dreshans have not been able to take this place,' he said.

'I will not make it to the Vandragamond if I stay here,' Zeralden had already made up her mind.

She entered the corridor that led to outside. 'You won't have any luck if you go there,' Tavion spoke, 'Follow me. If you want to leave you should avoid heading straight for the Dreshans.'

Her face grew red and she tried to hide it as she caught up with Tavion. He moved fast through the winding corridors as they passed other Arroada sorcerers. A narrow staircase led up along the north-west face of the hillside. She could make out the silhouette as the sky darkened into deep afternoon. When she turned back Tavion and any sign of the entrance, was gone.

CHAPTER THIRTEEN

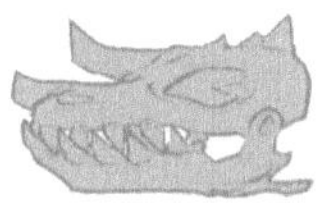

Toward the wizard Keep

A steady wind whipped around the edge of the woods and this time she stayed away from the path. The snow blanketed the ground with an even spread. The infant dragon was fast asleep snuggled in the rucksack. Any light had left the sky a while ago leaving her small circular talik to guide the way. It was enough to guide her steps as she used her sense to head toward Kaythar. It was still some distance away, and surrounded by open plains. She tried not to think of what would happen. Instead she placed one foot in front of the other. She concentrated on making it as far away from the Arroada stronghold as possible.

Her sorcery helped warm them, an owl hooted overhead marking the late night. She would have to find somewhere to stop soon, yet the words of the Keep lingered in her mind. The woods wrapped around a rocky hillside and she trailed toward it. The ground dipped into a small shelter, it was cosy, but large enough. Her shoulders ached as she let the rucksack rest. She curled up holding the Katholomu in her lap. Her sacra seal, the size of a coin, appeared minute as she wedged it in the ledge. Tiredness flooded and all she could do was close her eyes for sleep.

Kat wriggled toward her and licked her face, she nudged him in the rucksack and he purred. Then a loud rumbling purr echoed. Her eyes shot wide open and she glanced outside as the scales hid the stars from view. The full grown dragon fell against the entrance to the alcove blocking them in. She was too tired to worry about how to move it and let sleep set in.

The infant dragon sat making squawking noises at the large scales blocking the entrance. She doubted the large dragon took much notice if it was awake. Kat leaned up and scratched its side with his paws. 'We may be here for a while,' she explained.

She stretched her legs and gazed around the small space. Her stomach rumbled. All the walking from night before had given her an appetite and she reached into the sova bag. The smell of food caught the infant dragon's attention. He nibbled on a portion of dried meat.

Her muscles ached as she held the circular talik. Comparing the reading with the ragged map sprawled out on the ground. They were much closer than she anticipated, and that meant one thing. Soon they would reach open ground, her heart sank at the thought. She would need all her strength when all she wanted to do was rest. Katholomu climbed onto the side of the dragon and squeezed through the opening. She picked up the rucksack and held on the dragon's back making her way up.

It was not until she reached the top lying side ways to squeeze through. That she saw it was the dragon's tail. Relagrill turned his head to peer at the sorceress. His large eyes came close as tip of his nose snorted a warm acrid breath and she coughed. The giant of a marmoz dragon with his fine dark coat was one she recognised from Odana Temple. Large dragons had begun to return to the Keep before the attack. Even if the visits were fleeting. He dipped his head in greeting. Katholomu looked like a tiny spec in comparison as infant made his way up beside her.

She stood up and made her way along Relagrill's back. To the fold along his shoulders, but the dragon did not move. He searched the horizon waiting for something she could not see. As she peered down, she could tell he was tense and gathered her patience. Katholomu climbed between the large dragon's ears his body arched. The infant made her nervous, both dragons could sense something. She reached out her senses trying to find the source, yet none came.

A slim trail of dirt rained from above and Relagrill slammed his whole body into the hill. Zeralden glimpsed the Dreshan sorcerer's face before he went underneath the heavy dragon. The muffled sounds entered the air as Relagrill scraped hard against the rock. Heat emanated from his side. For a moment she thought it was the sorcerer until the dragon's belly grew wide. A great whoosh a flames thrust from his mouth melting the snow as it went. He shook free of the hill. She hesitated then stole a peek, but all that remained was the charred silhouette. 'Traitor,' the dragon spoke.

Then with a mighty jolt his muscles moved into a fluid run. The wings sprang upward slicing through the air. With one last jolt they were in the pale clear blue sky. She looked down at the dragon with his jet black coat the colour of night. If they had not been spotted they would be soon.

Relagrill headed straight for Kaythar Keep. The hills rolled in the underneath as her panic rose. She steadied her thoughts gazing along the ground. Every time she saw movement they passed by, the dragon was travelling at a swift pace. He flew straight path, every muscle filled with purpose as they picked speed. The rolling hills ebbed away and a scattering of villages crisscrossed the land. The fields covered in a white blanket as the winter sun held a crystal clear day. Her heart thudded in her ears as she held on tight. The villages led to the town. There looming at the northern end rising above the tallest hills was Kaythar Keep.

The great stone face of the Keep covered the town in shadow with morning light. Katholomu squawked peering behind. She glanced sideways to see the trail of dragons blotting the sky. The line filled the sky she turned around to see more to the right. Relagrill refused to acknowledge them flying hard toward the Keep. Yet it was still a distance away. The sky erupted from underneath as the flames of sorcery blasted the dragon's belly. Relagrill did not budge as he flew even harder toward the Keep.

Zeralden's energy rose. She had to defend the dragon, yet she had never faced protecting a moving target. She concentrated as the stream of blasts erupted below. The dragons were closing in fast from both directions. They were over the verge of the town. The Keep was in sight. A blast from the side sparked through the shield and hit Relagrill's wing. He dipped to the side and she clung on as he continued. A barrage of blasts hit from behind and the smell of burning flesh hit home. The dragon remained silent as he flew. They were almost there.

Relagrill veered sideways and she screamed as she fell. She rolled with a thud onto the platform of the Keep. The dragon threw all his rage toward the oncoming dragons. The sky filled with a fiery embrace. Wizards scattered in every direction, three Dreshan sorcerers stood on the platform. Tears flood her face as she held Alamere in the form of sword. She ran them through before they had a chance. As she turned all she could see was Relagrill falling from the sky.

CHAPTER FOURTEEN

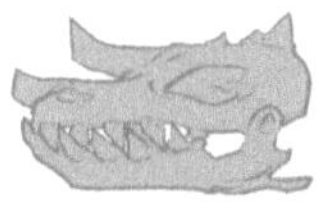

The dragon of time

She screamed letting the anguish escape as Relagrill hit the ground. Her bond-breaker clenched in her fist swayed in a wide arc. She called to the Keep reaching downward with her sorcery. The platform came to life as the glow of stallic energy ran across the surface. The energy stemmed from the central core hidden deep below. She raised the bond-breaker in both clutching it in both hands and waited. Just as the two flocks of dragons grouped. The ground erupted with mighty fire storm raging upward from where Relagrill had fallen.

The dragons that had been hit, shrieked sending panic through the line. It broke into chaos. She let the bond-breaker rest by her side, but she could not take her eyes from the sight. One of the greatest dragons in Zyanthia had given his life. Kat's growl broke her away and she turned.

The wizard closest to her stepped away almost losing his balance. One sorcerer remained on the open courtyard. He stood blocking the way into the Keep. 'All of Dresha will hunt you down,' he said.

He ignited the platform with his sorcery. It flared sending a brilliant array of storming through the clear sky.

Pain ripped through her body as Zeralden clung onto the bond-breaker Alamere. The blade sung with the blow and she held on. A rage swept over her so strong, yet it did nothing to stop the pain. She slammed the bond-breaker into the sorcerer's stone covering the platform and it shattered. The fine spray cut through time and space and nothing. It filled the void between the real world and the one of dreams. The energy from the Keep broke through the seals that confined its grip. Stallic energy, the energy of the Keep surged upward from the central core. A great rumbling pummelled from the depths below marking its rise toward the Angeon.

The few wizards ran for cover taking refuge along the outer rim. The Dreshan sorcerer's face grew pale as the Angeon rose from within Zeralden. She let the energy flow. A brief moment of calm wrapped around her isolating her from the outside world. Then the stallic energy hit taking the sorcerer to oblivion. It engulfed her and she clung on as the energy of the Keep melded with hers. One by one she searched for the Dreshans in the Keep. Kaythar raged with an excitement that bordered on hatred. As she hunted them using the energy from the Keep. The walls came to life and one by one fell to the keep.

As the last remnants faded she glided above the chasm that was the platform. In one final blast she projected her sorcery downward. The stallic energy cooled forming a perfect platform, one forged by the Angeon. Zeralden touched the surface. She sensed the heartbeat that was the central core. It hummed through the pathways that glided along forming tiny grooves. The Keep spoke, thank you. A noise cluttered the doorways leading to the courtyard. The Asdenard wizards gathered around. Raeborn held his arms wide and the group of wizards joined him. The shields surrounding Kaythar ignited over the settlement below.

Zeralden stood in silence watching, yet the no more dragon riders came. The day shone as though the morning had never been. She peered to the burnt crater where Relagrill had fallen. The dragon had given his life, and she felt that she had betrayed him. 'I have to leave,' she spoke aloud.

Raeborn responded, 'Are you going to fight your way out alone?'

She gave him a puzzled glance, and he explained, 'The Dreshan Army is here.'

Her face went pale as the wizards charged into action preparing the Keep.

Raeborn asked, 'Can you help with the shield?'

'Yes,' her voice was not convincing but there was no time.

She followed him into a small alcove. The floor gave way to a rush of air as the energy of the Keep whisked them downward. She had experienced the sensation at Odana

Temple. Yet the fall made her queasy as they floated before hitting the ground. Raeborn laughed and she glared at him. The Keep rumbled. It filled the open space hidden between arching frames below the habitable area. Light shone with an ambient glow from the ridge, the thick edge of the conduit came to her waist.

Raeborn leaned over as the Keep rumbled away. The sound weaved its way along the conduit from the core below. He waited, yet Zeralden hesitated. She had expected to a well-crafted connection and her heart sank. She peered into the empty void, all she saw were the walls of conduit leading below. Raeborn stood back in watching in silence. Kaythar called, it echoed up the conduit and the colour drained from her face. The wizard was standing to close. She hurried, trying to focus. The moments faded and the echo grew thundering up the conduit. She gazed upward the remainder of the conduit hidden well above the ceiling. A charred outline clung around the edges.

She cleared her mind and the energy of the Angeon rose to the surface. It hit the stallic energy rising from the core creating a smooth surface. 'Wow,' Raeborn whispered.

'Don't touch it,' she snapped.

As the two forms of energy met the conduit strengthened and joined once more. She gazed at the new surface and smiled with amazement. Raeborn asked, 'Can you do that again?'

She exclaimed, 'What?'

He grabbed her hand and they ran toward the next conduit.

She asked, 'How many are there?'

'Three,' he replied.

The Asdenard wizards darted out of their way. They ran through the tunnels and heavy frame that held the building above. She asked, 'Why are there so many?'

'This is where we live,' he answered.

Zeralden gasped, it was not what she expected. They ran toward the second conduit and the Keep was ready to greet them. He rumbled with eager anticipation. Kaythar met the energy of the Angeon to seal the broken link.

CHAPTER FIFTEEN

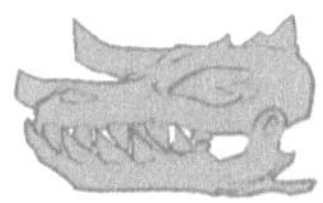

No rest for the unkind

They ran through the lower level of the Keep. Raeborn ducked and weaved around the great columns embedded in the walls. She did her best to keep up following as Katholomu glanced back. The infant dragon beckoned her, but it was not a game. Zeralden skidded across the floor. She almost fell straight over the jagged edge of the main conduit. She wanted to shout yet her voice came as a whisper. It merged with the rush of stallic energy stemming from inside the broken conduit. She concentrated catching the energy and melding it with hers. The outer circumference solidified. As the edges thickened and held in place she stood back.

The hum of the central core ignited filling the void as the room filled with light. Kaythar rumbled with excitement and they ran to the next conduit. She was beginning to doubt her own strength as she struggled to keep up. For all her days at Odana she had never needed to use so much energy. Raeborn stopped and the infant dragon skidded almost knocking the wizard off balance. She asked, 'What is it?'

'The conduit is through there,' Raeborn answered.

They stared at the debris blocking their path. Zeralden raised her arms. 'No,' he shouted, 'it could collapse.'

He pointed toward a small opening near the ceiling. 'Really,' she exclaimed.

Raeborn climbed up on the debris and helped her up. The narrow tunnel led between the floors. She could make out the narrow gap ahead and used her sorcery to light the way. The cobwebs clung to her sleeves, 'Do you live here?'

He turned and hesitated before answering, 'Yes.'

She managed to squeeze through the narrow opening. She placed her hand against the wall. The charred grime stuck and she wiped it off. 'Don't touch the walls, Raeborn said, 'this was used to execute the Arroada.'

She dry reached while trying not to touch the wall. The signs were plastered in blackened marks from floor to ceiling. 'You had to tell me,' she grimaced.

Kaythar gurgled from the deep, the sound echoed but the energy of the core did not rise. Zeralden paled, 'There is something down there.'

A thundering crackle rocked the building from above, it echoed through the gaping hole. She steadied herself calling the Angeon from within. She let it flow through her hands keeping it trapped as it grew. She let go and it ruptured. Lighting up the broken conduit with a fiery embrace as it sank into the depths. She tried not to think of what it would find. Kaythar rumbled and the stallic energy blew past her. She had not been ready but it had melded with the blast. The two combined to seal the main conduit. She released the breath that had frozen still.

Raeborn grabbed her hand and the Keep made an opening toward the last conduit. They ran through as the blasts shook the building, this time Kaythar answered. The great rumble exploded overhead, it rattled the foundations. Daylight seeped into the tunnel from the crumbled wall. A figure stood, the Dreshan sorcerer loomed overhead. The blade of his bond-breaker shone as he held it in an arc. There was no emotion on his face. Zeralden ran and Raeborn shouted, 'No. We have to fight.'

She turned in time to see the blade raised overhead. Raeborn blasted his energy toward the sorcerer who turned in one fluid motion. The sorcerer raised his energy, the liquid flame hurled in a straight path. Raeborn threw himself clear, yet the impact hit from the outer edge. She reached for her bond-breaker and swung it. The Dreshan sorcerer turned, his soulless eyes pierced her. Fear began to take hold, and she tried to focus. The Dreshan sorcerer, Ignatius, howled and she stammered back. The blade had not reached him yet he crumpled before regaining his composure.

It was then that she saw Evanna, the wizardess held her wizardry strong. Raeborn and several other wizards rushed in. He shouted above the noise, 'Hurry.'

His voice snapped her back to the reason why she had come. Zeralden ran to the last broken conduit. Her tired limbs rebelled against the flow of sorcery. Kaythar sealed in the main conduit. The rage that had been imprisoned in the depths swept to the surface. The Keep rumbled as she collapsed in a heap on the floor. Her face drained as the pain from using so much sorcery crept in. Evanna's cry cut through, she had forgotten about the Dreshan. Zeralden spun around as Evanna placed the cold steel band around the sorcerer's neck. The hyrik formed a perfect band of solid wizardry. Sitting so close to the skin it could trap sorcerer's energy inside.

She cringed at the thought, of being near the device and tried to speak. Her legs weakened and she gave in resting on the floor. Raeborn rushed over at first she could not hear his words. He asked again, 'Are you all right?'

She gave a faint nod and he helped to the makeshift quarters of the Asdenard. Her limbs felt heavy as she rested on the bed. She had done as much as she could and drifted into a heavy sleep.

The hum of Kaythar weaved its way into her mind. The Keep called from beneath a steady flow of stallic energy. That ran through the Keep strengthening the shield. She could sense it as she watched the wizards. They moved with a purpose. That made her wonder how long they had been waiting to regain their Keep. Raeborn spied her first and waved, he sat on the stool next to her. 'We have the Keep,' he spoke with eagerness.

'I need to get to the Vandragamond,' she spoke aloud

as she sat.

He asked, 'Have you seen yourself?'

Raeborn scrambled around for a mirror and held it up to her face. Her skin was almost white, and her lips gave a blue tinge. She hung her head in dismay, 'I have to go,' she said.

'You will only find death if you leave now,' a hint of worry clung to his voice.

She hated to admit it, but there was little she could do.

CHAPTER SIXTEEN

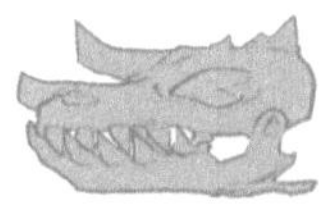

The path to a choice

Snow gathered around the base of the Keep. Kaythar kept the sorcerer army at bay yet it held her back. Zeralden needed to head north. Saving the wizard Keep had drained so much energy at once that she had to rest. Her mood had become irritable and the wizards avoided her with care. She peered over the edge of the sorcerers' stone. It stood high up on the main platform overlooking the north. The ice cold winds sent a chill streaming past. She pulled the cloak around her shoulders. Evanna read her immediate thoughts, 'You are welcome to stay.'

'If I make it back I will,' Zeralden was beginning to get nervous.

The greatest sorcerer clan in Zyanthia was so close, yet it was as though they did not exist. There had been no sign of them and she wondered if the Vandragamond knew she was at Kaythar. She asked, 'How far is it to the Keep Validain?'

Evanna glanced at the army settled near the hills on the horizon. 'A field deep of trouble,' she said.

Another day passed as Zeralden grew ever less patient. She had sent a message to the Vandragamond and there had been nothing. The silence became irritating and all she could do was plan and hope. As the Asdenard wizards settled their reluctance to take on the Dreshans. It left her in a whirlwind of her own thoughts as she hurried along. The infant dragon scurried to keep up. She leaned down and held Katholomu close. She searched through the equipment stored below ground. A scream cut through the air and took her breath away. She ran in the direction of the wizards, Ignatious stood before them. The charred remnants of the hyrik lay scattered on the ground.

Evanna gave a scream of pain then the Dreshan sorcerer's eyes glazed. He fell against the wall. Zeralden let her sorcery build and Raeborn shouted, 'No. This is not your place.'

'But…' She interrupted.

He held her arm and they moved away. She waited hoping for an explanation, 'You cannot interfere with a bond.'

Her face went pale at the thought, 'He can't.'

'It's happened. Now we are bound to recognise it,' Raeborn emphasised the word 'we'.

It was the last thing she expected as Raeborn did his best to keep her away. The Dreshan sorcerer that had tried to kill her would be let loose to wonder the Kaythar. She tried not to think about it. Somehow she had to find a way to leave without facing the Dreshan Army. Yet her senses could find them gathered along the perimeter of the wizard Keep. The Asdenard were grateful to have their building returned. Yet that did not extend to helping her. She strode along the corridor overlooking the north. She peered through its arched windows amidst the columns. The warmth of the central core kept the cold at bay. The sun shone down a blanket of white snow trimming the fields.

One more battle to fight and she would find the Vandragamond. They were the greatest sorcerer clan in Zyanthia. She had to leave. The thought consumed her as she searched her belongings scattering them across the bed. Katholomu pounced playing a game, stepped on the map before she had a chance to hold it. The only hint she could find was the one she had been taught at Odana. Call the Vandragamond and they will come. It made almost no sense as she sat in frustration. She waited until the sun lowered in the sky. Marking the afternoon as the darkness of winter gripped the land. The infant dragon scurried near her feet as they made their way out into the cold dim air.

'Eager to leave,' the voice sent a chill down her spine.

Ignatious leaned with his back to the wall. She glared at him in an irrefutable silence. He continued, 'I am intrigued as to how you intend to fight an army.'

'Shouldn't you be somewhere,' she retorted.

He gave a sly grin, 'I am where I need to be.'

She strode onward. Along the stone path that led away from the protection of the wizard Keep. Ignatious shouted after her, 'Do you know why Vandragamond do not answer?'

She gave him a cold stare as a chill wind gained ground, 'Why?'

'They made a deal with Dresha,' he responded.

She fumed yet she could not waste time with the sorcerer. His words filled her with a deep frustration. The great Keep began to shrink as she made her way toward the furthest end node. It was the last saving grace while heading north. Without it she would be vulnerable. If she was to be the Angeon she would have to be one now more than ever. Katholomu rested in the rucksack as she stood covered by a heavy coat. It took the edge off the chill and her sorcery kept her warm. She peered up to the sky as the night fell still, the rucksack slid off with ease. She took off the coat, the last sign of comfort as the ice cold wind whipped against her skin.

There was one thing Arkimous had taught her in the depths of Odana Temple. The one skill no one dared speak of for fear of what the Angeon would do. It was a skill that remained unspoken, hidden in the walls of Odana. Yet Arkimous had taught her knowing it could end his life if he had been found out. It seemed insignificant in the heart of winter. The temple was but a memory as she held out her hands. The sorcerer's stone sealing the end node in a circular tome. It began to merge as the ground swirled.

At first it took all her might with slow turn. Then it

gathered speed plunging into the ground. As the stone dipped to form a gaping hole she stayed floating above the vortex. So far from the central core the Angeon appeared in the darkness. She floated above the tunnel leading into the depths of Tordoren. Zeralden rose high into the night sky and with the strength of the whirlwind below. She took the first strike against the army that had shattered Zyanthia.

CHAPTER SEVENTEEN

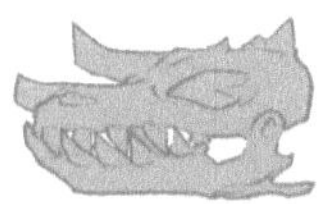

Battle to the end of days

Lightening shot across the void in a sweeping curve spreading out in a web. The arc was fatal as it crashed into the ground. It shot across the night sky in a cascading avalanche. As the thunderstorm took held she fell, the whirlwind closed beneath. At the last moment she floated kneeling on the sorcerer's stone. Zeralden had given everything to distract the Dreshan Army. She picked up her coat and the rucksack running as hard as she could. There was only one chance, one the Army realised where she was she would have to face them alone. She held Alamere her bond-breaker in the form of a dagger, gripping it in the palm of her hand.

The dark sky hid her in the panic across the open ground. Yet all it would take was one Dreshan, she kept the thought from entering her mind as she ran. The great dragons ran through scattering the crowd of sorcerers. She dodged the shrieking dragon as the smell of charred flesh lay pungent in the air. The ground shook as it hit hard, a voice cried out and a sorcerer began to turn toward her. Jule screeched above the noise, 'Angeon.'

A surge of energy flared from behind her. She weaved around a sorcerer only just avoiding the blast. The crowd gathered in amid the confusion yet it took time through the chaos. She ran hoping to reach the edge. As she gazed north the outer rim of soldiers fell into place blocking her in. The high tower of Keep Validain loomed in the distance offering a beacon to guide her. Yet the Vandragamond remained silent, as though they did not exist. The Dreshan Army circled in. She slowed glancing around as the group tightened around her. Gorran stood almost motionless glaring at her from the circle.

The Dreshan Army ceased their advance yet there was no way out. An eerie moment of solitude clung in the air as the army gathered closing ranks. Their sorcery bound together as Zeralden changed her bond-breaker to the form of sword. Alamere shone in the dark, a deep sea green. Gorran raised his bond-breaker. Three other sorcerers did the same yet still they did not move closer. A hum rose through the army and she went pale, sensing the sorcery of the Dreshans rise. It took all her concentration to hold it back. Gorran took aim in a sweeping arc. She almost hesitated under the strain as she deflected the bond-breaker.

Gorran swung wide with an arrogant certainty and

she took the plunge. Alamere pierced through his arm and he riled in pain. The Dreshan sorcery began to rise as she lost her concentration. The first wave ripped along the edge of her senses and she plunged to the ground. The rucksack fell from her shoulder. Gorran yelled as Katholomu bit into the wound. Zeralden glanced up to see dragon riders' swarm from the direction of Kaythar Keep. The pain set in when she tried to move, the Dreshans were blocking her in. A great flame shot from the first dragon swooping from the sky. The infant dragon answered.

A huff of smoke roared into flame and she surged her energy toward the hatchling. The spark hit true, igniting the sorcery that held her tight. She picked up Kat and ran, the infant dragon held out his wings spurring her on. He growled as Zeralden shielded their path. The dragon riders arrived, their formation a perfect line adding flame to the chaos. She focused on pearl towers of Validain glimmering in the light. The cold crept in as she broke past the edge of the army's might. The Vandragamond were so close yet still there was no sign.

Snow coated the hillside making the path hazardous. She tried to run but it would not relent. The bitter wind sent a chill through her thick cloak. Katholomu nestled into the rucksack. His eyes peered just above the opening watching every move. The rocky hillside proved much harder than she anticipated. She carried on until a makeshift shelter beckoned. It was a risked she had to take, her hands were ice cold and exhaustion had set in. Katholomu bounced from the warmth of the rucksack and stood guard. She set the sacra seal and hoped it would be enough. Every muscle ached, reminding her of what could have been.

She rested her weary head yet the images that seeped through into her dreams. Were of the Dreshan Army blocking her escape. Her body screamed for sleep yet the image held her. It woke her through the dark of morning and into the first rays of light. She could hardly move and willed her muscles to give. Katholomu hurried her then hid in the rucksack as they left. The quiet morning hid all signs of the night before and she made her way along the icy path. The gravel turned to stone and widened making the journey easier.

Tiny flecks of snow floated down. She made her way toward the high wall guarding the outer rim of the Keep. The great divide between Zyanthia and the clan Vandragamond stood silent. It loomed into the sky. A gap marking the way in, remained deserted as though the clan did not exist. She hesitated, it was the first time she had ever doubted what Arkimous told her. What of the sorcerer clan did not exist? The thought was too much and she rushed the last distance to the gateway. It was in reach, and she held out her hand. As it passed through the gateway the shield shone yet it let her pass.

The streets were empty as though the clan had vanished before she arrived. She strode toward the centre, toward Validain. The sorcerer Keep shone radiant with a white pearl façade. It glowed in the morning sun. As she glanced around there was no sign of struggle or war. Her anxiety grew the closer she came to the great building. The stairs ran horizontal creating a wide platform Katholomu ran ahead leading the way. The view caught her attention. She turned gazing straight into the eyes of the Vandragamond.

CHAPTER EIGHTEEN

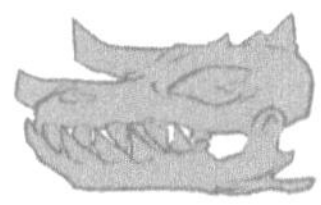

The rise of the sorcerer lord

In one glance the image broke on the edge of her sight and the two worlds met as she saw through the haze. The ripple ran through the clan as the thin line between time and space collided. Zeralden drew her bond-breaker Alamere as the phase melted away. Meldrick stood on the platform surrounded by the clan. The thick dark fur wrapped around his shoulders hiding the bulk of his armour. The horns from his helmet cast a dark shadow across the stone. It was a replica of the sorcerers that gathered around. Without thinking she took a step back. The infant dragon growled standing between her and the clan.

Meldrick roared with laughter, 'Is this your mighty dragon.'

She glared at him, 'Katholomu took down Gorran…'

She was about to explain and the sorcerer interrupted,

'I know who Gorran is.'

The question blurted out before she could stop. 'Did you make a deal with the Dreshans?' She asked.

He gave a vague response, 'you will have to ask the High Lord little Angeon.'

The infant dragon backed away as Meldrick led them into the sorcerer Keep. The clan wore their weapons in the open without fear. Zeralden placed Alamere away and followed the infant dragon.

The great hall loomed ahead, voices and noise travelled along the open walkway. A sorcerer screamed in pain yet as she stride in the clan hid any remnant of the scene. High Lord Kagan sat in plain wooden chair taller than the rest at the end of the vast room. His grey wisps of remaining hair escaped from the edges of his helmet, yet he did not speak. The administrator Alesia stood by his side wearing the robes of her station. It was not the encounter Zeralden had imagined. She strode up the High Lord, 'Did you make a deal with Dresha?'

A thin smile appeared on his lips. Alesia answered, 'We do not make deals with heathen.'

Lord Kagan spoke, 'Is that what you came here for? Little Angeon you have a lot to learn.'

She explained, 'Arkimous sent me…'

'Arkimous is dead, before that he was a fool,' the Lord said.

He stood, Meldrick and Alesia followed. They made their way along the wide walkway. To an elegant tower crowned by a glorious pearl dome. The columns stretched downward marking the size of the structure.

Lord Kagan waited for the doors of the grand chamber to open. They went inside hidden from remainder of the clan. 'Many years ago a young man travelled to Validain. He sought audience with the Vandragamond,' he said. 'He claimed he would defend Zyanthia if we offered him our agreement.'

The High Lord stood in the centre of the grand chamber. He faced her, 'I offered that agreement to the Angeon who resides with the Shalough. As long as he lives the agreement will stand.'

Tears began to trickle down her face, and Zeralden shouted, 'No. You lie.'

'We stay at Validain,' the Lord responded.

'Coward,' she spat the word at him.

Zeralden gripped the bond-breaker Alamere. 'It will not help,' Lord Kagan spoke, 'This is where journey ends.'

She shouted as the Angeon rose inside, 'This is where your journey begins.'

The blade shimmered with the sea green heart stone of Odana Temple. She held it up the pearl dome ceiling. The stallic energy of the Keep rose to great her. She ran toward the High Lord holding the blade to the sky. The small Orb held in the centre of the hilt shone bright, Lord Kagan did not move. In the void between time and space Zeralden reached out with the energy of the Angeon. She severed the bond between the Lord and Hallam. Lord Kagan let out a silent scream as he fell to his knees on the floor of the grand chamber.

She let the stallic energy sink back into the central core, and held Alamere close. 'Arkimous was no fool,' she shouted in disgust.

She watched as the High Lord struggle to his feet. 'You hid from the Dreshans and let Zyanthia burn. You are not worthy to be called Vandragamond,' she said.

She stormed from the grand chamber. The clan watching her as she strode long the walkway. 'Little Angeon,' Alesia called out, 'You will have your Zyanthia.'

At first the words had no meaning then Validain shone golden in mid-day sun. Stallic energy ran through it from the central core. It came to life with the greatest sorcerer clan, the Vandragamond. Lord Kagan marched toward her. 'You don't know how long I have waited.' He shouted to the clan, 'Today we fight.'

Zeralden gripped her bond-breaker, 'I will fight with you.'

ACKNOWLEDGEMENTS

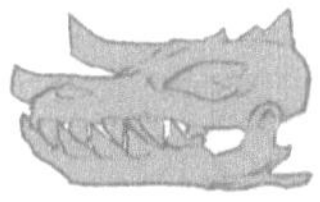

Life has been a journey filled with many challenges, and the people I would like to thank would not fit on this page. To everyone out there who has been part of this incredible journey thank you, your support has been appreciated.

– Please Leave a Review –

For all the wonderful people who have read the book it would be fantastic if you can leave a review, this helps other readers find it. Thank you.

BOOKS

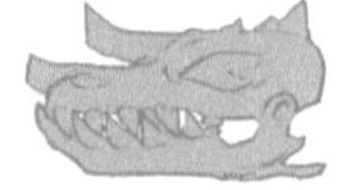

The Legacy of Zyanthia series:
Made in the Image of the Goddess
Running through the Rising Tide
Deep in the Shadow of the Fallen
Challenging the Fires of Chaos

Legends of Zyanthia:
Battle to the End of Days

AUTHOR

If you love fantasy with adventure and a hint of the unexpected the quest is about to begin. Escape into fantasy, and the mystical world of magic mixed with adventure. You are in good company although chose your company wisely. There are anti-heroes, wizards, and a range of chaotic characters ahead. Not to mention dragons. A fantasy world set in an ancient mythical world has to have dragons. Tales of sword and sorcery captivated Chantelle from a young age. Reading until all hours of the night to find out what would happen to the characters. There was just one problem the story would finish far too soon.

Hidden away in the distant past the life of a fantasy writer began. The real life struggles have been a saga all of their own for author Chantelle Griffin born in Tasmania, Australia. Her dreams haunted her from an early age. Vivid tumultuous dreams carrying adventure and danger. It took the author into a fantasy world filled with sorcery and treachery. The story continues to captivate her writing. If you love fantasy with adventure follow the Legacy of Zyanthia series.

www.chantellegriffin.com

GLOSSARY

ANGEON: 'The Angeon is Darkonia's answer to the Oracle, a sorcerer born with the ability to break down all defences and render a civilisation powerless.' There had been no Angeon since shortly after the Dreshan Occupation ended over 200 years ago with Zeralden Hadenvar the last Angeon who ruled Darkonia (as Queen) by marriage to the King's second son.

BOND-BREAKER: A weapon made by sorcery when dormant resembles a dagger, when activated resembles a sword it acts as a catalyst to magnify and aim the user's energy and can be used equally well by wizards as well as sorcerers. 'The most feared swords a sorcerer could use made of heart stone a melding of the elements to form a solid material that resembled crystal and sharp enough to cut through stone.'

CENTRAL CORE: The working core mechanism which powers the Keep, usually hidden away deep within the earth. It is a large engine created by sorcery which then continues to thrive on a combination of energy drawn from deep within the earth and sorcery. The combination creates a very raw and powerful energy which is difficult to manipulate.

DEAD ZONE: This is created when part of the Keep is not receiving energy from the central core or when energy has been diverted.

END NODE: Last outpost of a Keep's main energy source located at semi-regular intervals around the perimeter.

FERMADICIDE: Dark skeletal creatures.

FIRE MARK: A mark on the right shoulder to, the symbol of the fires of chaos given to the Issola in the camps.

HILAZEN: Bonded wizard.

HOST: Wizard joined with a Keep, it takes 60 hours to complete a union.

HYRIK: Restraint on sorcery, like a collar.

IMBENIK CHAMBER: Near the central core within the Keep, in between the indolin chamber and the central core it contains alters where a sorcerer can meld with the Keep.

INDOLIN CHAMBER: Inside the Keep, in between the habitable area and the central core.

KEDRIL(S): Tools to fix a Keep.

KEEP: A building protected by a central core powered by sorcery and energy from the earth. 'The tunnels led down to the primary systems and the central core that transferred energy from far below the ground into the core and turned into a usable energy source. Most central cores were located deep in the ground where the temperature was constantly warm…'

KULTIER: Long giant cockroaches.

LAY-LINE: Fast method of travel.

MAZETTE: Small (bird size) dragons.

MISQUEW: Riding cat.

NEFRELLE: Small creature (cat size), part human with very sharp teeth and claws.

OCKREN: Big cat, the soul of the Keep.

PALAFON: Tiny dragon.

QUADMAR: Aquatic creature from the murky depths, larger than a mermaid.

SACRA SEAL: Small, can hold it on your hand.

SHEAL: Liquid inside the Keep, very potent compressed raw energy.

SKADA: Small mechanical creatures that help maintain the Keep, they resemble a large spider.

SOVA BAG: A deceptive small light pouch that can become an enormous bag and hold a lot of objects, it will not hold living things.

STALLIC ENERGY: Energy from the Keep.

TALIK: Communication device. 'The sorceress held up her talik a small round disc that could open small enough to fit in the palm of her hand and placed her thumb on the centre of the outside…'

TRIDEN: Giant crab/spider, dark brown.

UVALEN CODE: '…A complex masterpiece describing the natural laws that governed sorcery.'

ZENNIGH: A large cat that normally lives within a Keep, they are too big to fit in a house but that has not stopped the occasional one from trying and getting their head jammed in the doorway.

ZYANTHIAN REGION: Armedicia, Taria, Normisia, Darkonia and Alveron were formed from one country called Zyanthia.